CELTIC
FAIRY TALES

CELTIC
FAIRY TALES

RETOLD BY PHILIP WILSON

Illustrated by
Sue Clarke, Anna Cynthia Leplar, Jacqueline Mair,
Sheila Moxley, and Jane Tattersfield

mustard

First published in 1999 by Mustard
Mustard is an imprint of Parragon

Parragon
Queen Street House
4 Queen Street
Bath BA1 1HE

Created by
The Albion Press Ltd
Spring Hill, Idbury, Oxfordshire OX7 6RU

ISBN 1-84164-199-5

A copy of the British Library Cataloguing in Publication Data
is available from the British Library.

Typeset by York House Typographic, London
Colour origination by Inka Graphics, Cardiff
Printed and bound in Italy by Olivotto

Contents

The Tale of Ivan

Ivan was a poor man who had no work. So one day he left his wife to look for a job. After a while he came to a farm and the farmer agreed to take Ivan on and give him lodgings.

Ivan worked on the farm for a year, and the master said, "Ivan, you have worked well this year. It is now time for you to be paid. Will you be paid in money or advice?"

"I would prefer to take my wages in money," said Ivan.

"I would prefer to give you advice," said the master. "Never leave the old road for the new one." So Ivan had to be content with this piece of advice, and worked for his master another year.

At the end of the second year, the same thing happened. This time, the master told Ivan, "Never lodge where an old man is married to a young woman." Again Ivan had to be content with the advice.

After a third year, the master gave Ivan a third piece of advice, "Honesty is the best policy." By now, Ivan saw that he would get no money from this master, so he decided to take his leave and return to his wife. Maybe there would be work

nearer home.

"Very well," said the master. "I will give you a cake to eat on your journey."

Ivan set off and soon he fell in with a group of merchants who were returning home from a fair. He got on well with the merchants, but when they came to a fork in the road, the men wanted to travel along the shorter, straighter, new road. Ivan remembered his master's first piece of advice. "I prefer the old road," said Ivan, and they parted company.

Before long, the merchants were set upon by robbers. Ivan

could see what was happening, for the new road was visible from the old. "Robbers! Stop thief!" he bellowed at the top of his voice. When the robbers heard this, they ran off, and the merchants kept hold of their money.

After many miles, the two roads joined again near a market town, and before long Ivan had met the merchants once more. "Thank you for saving us from the robbers," said one of them. "We will pay for your night's lodgings."

"I'll see the host first," said Ivan when they got to the inn. Ivan found out that the inn was owned by an old man with a young wife. He remembered his master's advice. "I'll not lodge here," he said, and while the merchants settled down to a meal of roast pork, Ivan took a room in the house next door.

Now it so happened that the young wife of the old landlord was plotting with a young monk to kill her husband and take over the inn. They saw that if they did the crime that night they could pin the blame on the merchants, who were the only guests. The pair were preparing to carry out their wicked plan in an upper room of the inn where the old man was sleeping. But they did not know that Ivan, getting ready to go to bed in his room next door, could hear them through the wall. There was a missing pine knot in the wall and Ivan looked through and saw them talking.

Suddenly, the young woman saw the hole in the wall. "We

must block that hole," she said, "or someone may see us." So the monk stood hard against the hole while the wicked woman stabbed her husband to death.

Ivan saw his chance. He took his knife and cut out a piece of the monk's habit while he stood against the hole.

In the morning, the crime was discovered and the wife went screaming to the justices. "It must have been that gang of wicked merchants staying at the inn," she cried. The merchants were marched off to prison, and Ivan saw them pass.

"Woe to us, Ivan!" they cried. "Our luck is running out. We are taken for this murder, but we are all innocent."

"Tell them to find the real murderers," called Ivan.

"But no one knows who committed the crime," said one of the merchants.

"If I cannot bring them to justice," said Ivan, "let them hang *me* for the murder."

So Ivan went to the justices and told them everything he had heard. At first, the justices did not believe him, but when he showed them the piece of cloth he had cut from the monk's robe, they knew it must be true, and the young wife and the monk were arrested. The merchants were released, thanked Ivan for his trouble, and went on their way.

When Ivan got home to his wife she ran to greet him. "You come in the nick of time," she said. "I have just found a fine purse of gold. It has no name on it, but it must belong to the lord of the manor."

"Honesty is the best policy," said Ivan, remembering the third piece of advice. "Let us take it to the lord's house."

When they got to the lord's castle, they left the purse with the servant at the gatehouse.

One day, the lord passed Ivan's house, and his wife mentioned the purse to him. "I know of no purse returned to me," said the lord, in puzzlement. "Surely my servant must have kept it for himself."

Off they went to the castle and sought out the servant. As soon as the lord accused him, the servant saw that he was

found out, and gave up the purse. The lord frowned at his wicked servant. "I have no use for dishonest men. Be gone from my castle," he ordered.

Then the lord turned to Ivan. "Will you be my servant in his place?"

"Thank you," said Ivan. And he and his wife were given fine new quarters in the castle. When they were moving in, Ivan remembered the cake his old master had given him. They cut themselves a piece, and out fell three gold coins, Ivan's wages for his work for his old master. "Truly, honesty is the best policy," laughed Ivan. And his wife agreed.

Cherry of Zennor

Near the village of Zennor in Cornwall lived a man everyone called Old Honey. With him in his tiny two-room hut lived his wife and ten children. They managed with the little living space they had, and grew what food they could on the land around the hut, adding limpets and periwinkles, which they gathered from the shore.

Old Honey's favourite daughter was Cherry, who could run as fast as the wind. She was always mischievous, but had such a winning smile that everyone liked her. She loved to steal the horse of the miller's boy when he came into the village, and would ride out to the cliffs. If the miller's boy seemed to be catching up, she would leave the horse behind, and hide in the rocks or cairns that there were along the coast, and neither the miller's boy nor any other could catch her or find her.

Cherry was a sweet-natured child, but when she reached her teens she became discontented. She wanted so much to have a new dress, so that she could cut a fine figure at church or at the fair. But there was no money for dresses, so she had to mend the one she had. She thought it was not fit for her to go

to the fair and look for a sweetheart.

One day, Cherry decided that she would leave home and look for a job, so that she might have money of her own. So the next morning she wrapped her few possessions in a bundle and set off. On she trudged, but when she came to the cross roads at Lady Downs, she sat down on a stone and cried, for she felt tired, missed her family, and wished she had not set out on her own.

Just as she was drying her eyes and deciding that she would return to her family, a gentleman appeared. Cherry thought this was odd, since she had seen no one coming before, and on the Downs you could see for miles around. When the man bid her "Good morning," Cherry told him that she had left home to seek her fortune, but that she had lost heart and was going to return.

"I did not expect such good luck," said the man. "I am looking for a young woman to come and keep house for me, for I am recently a widower." So Cherry decided that she would go with the man, and they set off across the Downs together.

As they went, the gentleman told Cherry that she would have little to do but milk the cow and look after his small son. He did not live far away, he said, explaining that his home was in the "low country", the valley beyond the Downs. After a while they walked into an area where the lanes were sunk deep into the ground, with trees and bushes growing high on either side. Little sunlight reached the lane where they walked, but there was a rich scent of sweetbrier and honeysuckle, and these pleasant scents reassured Cherry, who might otherwise have been afraid of the dark.

Next they came to a river, and the gentleman picked Cherry up around the waist and carried her across. On the other side, the lane seemed even darker, and Cherry held the man's arm.

Soon they came to the gentleman's home. When she saw the place, Cherry could not believe her eyes. The dark lane had not prepared her for a place of such beauty. The garden was full of flowers of every colour, fruit of all descriptions hung down from the trees, and birds sat in the branches, singing as if they were pleased that the master of the house had come home.

The garden was so unlike her own home that Cherry remembered how her grandmother had told her of places that had been enchanted by the little people. Could this be such a place?

Cherry looked up as a voice called "Papa!" and a small child, about two or three years old, came rushing towards the gentleman. But when Cherry looked at the child, although he was small, his faced seemed old and wrinkled. She was about to speak to the child when a haggard old woman appeared out of the house and came towards them.

"This is Aunt Prudence, my late wife's grandmother," said the gentleman. He explained that the old woman would stay until Cherry had learned her work, then she would leave.

When they went indoors, Cherry found that the house was even more beautiful than its garden. Aunt Prudence produced a large and tasty meal, and they all sat down to eat, after which the old woman showed Cherry to her room.

"When you are in bed, keep your eyes closed," said Aunt Prudence. "If you open your eyes, you may see things that frighten you." Then she explained what work Cherry would have to do the next day. She was to take the boy to the spring and wash him, after which she was to rub some ointment into his eyes. She would find the ointment in a box hidden in a gap in the rock by the spring. On no account should she put the ointment on her own eyes. Then she was to call the cow and milk her, and give the boy milk for his breakfast.

The following morning, Cherry rose early and began her work. She went with the little boy to the spring, where she washed him and put the ointment on his eyes. Then she looked around for the cow, but could see no beast anywhere. So Cherry made a clicking noise, which she had used when calling the cows in Zennor, and suddenly a fine cow appeared from among the trees, and Cherry sat down to milk her.

After breakfast, the old woman showed Cherry everything in

the kitchen. Then Aunt Prudence told Cherry that under no
circumstances should she try to go into any of the locked
rooms in the house. "You might see something that would
frighten you," she repeated. After this warning, Cherry went
out to help her master in the garden. She and the gentleman
got on well, but Cherry did not like the old woman, who was
often hovering around in the background, muttering, as if she
did not like the girl and wanted her gone.

  When Cherry seemed settled in her new home, Prudence
said, "Now you shall see some parts of the house you have not
seen before." One room had a floor that was polished like glass
and around all the walls were figures of men, women, and

children, all made of stone. They looked to Cherry as if they were real people who had somehow been turned to stone, and she shivered with fear as she looked at them.

Poor Cherry thought she had come into a house of wicked conjurors, and looked at the old woman in fear. "I don't want to see any more," she said.

But the old woman laughed, and pushed Cherry into another room, where she was made to polish a large box that looked like a coffin on legs. "Rub harder, harder!" shouted the old woman, with a look of madness in her eyes, and as Cherry

rubbed, she heard an awful wailing sound, which chilled her to the bone. The girl fainted as she heard it, and the master burst into the room.

When he saw what had happened, the gentleman threw the old woman out of the house, shouting that she should never have shown Cherry the locked room. Then he gave Cherry a soothing drink to revive her. It made Cherry feel better, and it also made her forget exactly what she had seen. But she knew that she had been frightened, and that she did not want to go into that part of the house again.

Life was much better for Cherry with the old woman gone. She was happy in her master's house, but still curious about what was going on there. One day, when her master was out, she decided to try some of the child's ointment on her own

eyes. As she rubbed in the ointment, she felt a terrible burning and dashed to the pool under the rock to splash cool water on her eyelids. As she did so, she saw hundreds of tiny people at the bottom of the pool – and among them was her master!

The ointment had given Cherry the ability to see the little people, and when she looked, she could see them everywhere, hiding in the flowers, swinging in the trees, running around under blades of grass. Another time, she saw her master playing with a host of the little people. One of them, dressed up like a queen, was dancing on top of the coffin, and the master took her in his arms and kissed her.

Next day, when Cherry and her master were together in the garden, he bent to kiss her. This was enough for Cherry. "Kiss the little people like yourself, as you do when you go under the water," she cried, and slapped her master on the face. The gentleman knew that Cherry had used some of the ointment on her eyes. She would have to leave him for good.

Sadly, Cherry and her master parted. He gave her a bundle full of clothes and other fine things, picked up a lantern, and led her away from his garden, along the sunken lanes, and towards the Downs. Then he gave the girl a final kiss, and said with a hint of sadness in his voice that he was sorry, but that

she must be punished for her curiosity. Perhaps he would see her sometimes if she walked upon the Downs.

So Cherry returned to Zennor. Her people were surprised to see her, for she had been away for so long, without sending news of her whereabouts, that they had thought she was dead. When she told her story to her parents, they could not believe it at first, and thought she was telling it to cover up some mischief that she had been part of. But Cherry insisted that her story was true, and in time her family accepted what she said. Often she wandered on the Lady Downs, looking for her old master. But she never saw him again.

Skillywidden

A man was cutting furze on Trendreen Hill one fine day, and he saw one of the little people stretched out, fast asleep, on the heath. The man took off the thick cuff that he wore at his work, crept up quietly, and popped the little man into the cuff before he could wake up. Then he carried his find home with care, and let the creature out on to the hearth stone.

When he awoke, the fairy looked quite at home and soon began to enjoy himself playing with the children. They called him Bob of the Heath, and Bob told the man that he would show him where to find crocks of gold hidden on the hillside.

Several days later, the neighbours joined together to bring away the harvest of furze, and all came to the man's house to celebrate the end of their task with a hearty meal. To hide Bob away from prying eyes, the man locked him in the barn with the children.

But the fairy and his playmates were cunning, and soon found a way out of the barn. Before long they were playing a game of dancing and hide-and-seek all around the great heap of furze in the yard.

As they played, they saw a tiny man and woman searching round the furze. "Oh my poor Skillywidden," said the tiny woman. "Where can you be? Will I ever set eyes on you again?"

"Go back indoors," said Bob to the children. "My mother and father have come looking for me. I must go back with them now." Then he cried, "Here I am mummy!" And before the children knew what had happened, their playmate Bob had vanished with his parents, and they were left in the yard.

When they told their father what had happened, the man was angry, and gave them a beating for escaping from the locked barn.

After this the furze-cutter sometimes went to Trendreen Hill to look for fairies and crocks of gold. But he was never able to find either.

Tom and the Giant Blunderbuss

Long ago, when the world was ruled by giants, there was a young giant called Tom. Although he was young and strong, Tom was a lazy lad who spent most of the time mooching around with his hands in his pockets. Now and then, Tom would spring into action, and would move dozens of massive boulders to build a wall, just to show what he could do if he tried. But usually he was idle.

Tom's mother grew sick of her son's idleness, and after much nagging, persuaded him to take a job driving a brewer's wagon. Tom thought that if he had to have a job, this would be a good one, because at least he would be able to get plenty to drink. So off he went to live in the nearest market town, where he began to work for the brewer.

One day he was out with his wagon when he came across a group of men trying to lift a fallen tree. They seemed to be making a poor effort of it, so he stopped, helped them, and in a trice had lifted the tree where they wanted it. The men thanked him, and he set off again along the road to St Ives.

After a while, Tom came to a place where a wall blocked the road. Tom knew that the lands behind the wall belonged to a great giant known as Blunderbuss. Many years before, the road had gone straight ahead, but now it was blocked by Blunderbuss's wall. If the giant had not lived there, Tom could have gone straight on in the direction of St Ives. But as it was, he would have to go a long way round.

Tom looked at the giant's gate and wondered whether he should take the short cut through. But the giant had a cruel reputation. He had married several times, and people said that he had killed each of his wives. Tom therefore thought better of trespassing on the giant's land, and carried on his journey by the normal road.

But on his way back, Tom was tired and full with the four gallons of beer he had drunk at St Ives, and he decided to take the shorter route home. So he drove his wagon through the giant's great gate and across the field where the giant's cattle grazed contentedly. When he had gone about a mile, he arrived at a gate in a high wall which surrounded the giant's castle.

The only way was forward, so Tom pushed open the gate and began to drive his oxen across the castle courtyard. As he went along, Tom heard some dogs barking loudly, and then the great giant himself emerged from his castle.

"What are you doing driving into my castle courtyard and disturbing my afternoon sleep?" roared the giant.

"I am on the right road," said Tom. "You have no right to stop me going home."

"I will not trouble myself to argue with a saucy young rascal like you," said Blunderbuss. "I shall fetch a twig and beat you to my gate."

The giant pulled up an elm tree taller than three men and began to strip the branches from the trunk. He still seemed to be half asleep, but he could do this without any effort at all. Tom saw what he was doing, and looked around for a weapon to defend himself. His eye lighted on his wagon, so he pulled out one of the axles, took one of the wooden wheels as a shield, and stood ready for the giant's blows.

Blunderbuss rushed at Tom, but Tom dodged quickly, the ground was slippery, and the giant squelched into the mud. Tom could have killed the giant easily when he was down, but the young lad thought that this was unfair. So he merely tickled Blunderbuss in the ribs with his axle, and said, "Up you get. Let's have another turn."

Quickly, Blunderbuss got up and rushed at Tom without warning. But Tom was ready for him, and held out his axle so that it pierced the giant's body right through. Blunderbuss gave out a dreadful roar.

"Stop bleating like a sheep!" said Tom. "I will pull out my

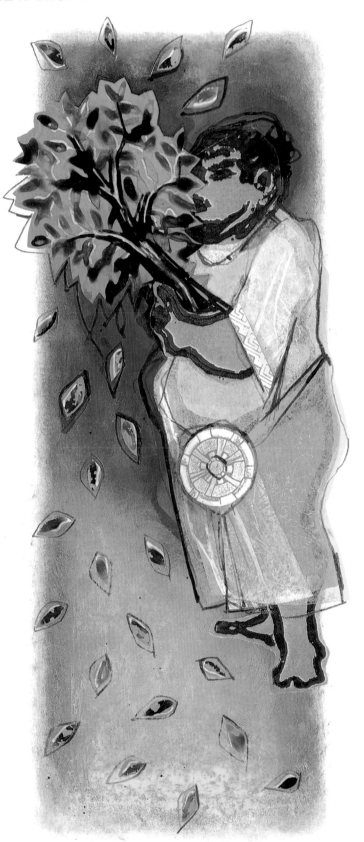

axle, then we can have another turn."

But when he withdrew his weapon, Tom saw that blood was pouring from the giant's wound. Tom cut some turf and gave this to the giant to plug the hole, and then Tom was ready to fight once more. But the giant Blunderbuss held up his hand. "No, I can fight no more. You have wounded me mortally. And you have done well, fighting bravely even when I tried to trick you by rushing at you when you were not prepared. I would like to do you some good, for you are the only one who has

been brave enough to stand up to me. Listen carefully. I have no near relations and I want you to have my wealth and my lands when I die. In my castle cellar, two dogs guard my gold.

The dogs are called Catchem and Tearem. If you go into the cellar they will attack you unless you call them by their names. Simply do this and you can take the gold."

Tom listened in silence as the giant told him of the wealth and lands that he would own. In the end he asked, "Did you kill your wives?"

"No. They died of natural causes. Please do not let people tell lies about me when I am dead."

And Tom was about to reassure the giant and tell him that his time was not yet come, when Blunderbuss closed his eyes, and all was over.

Tom went back home with his wagon, but returned to the giant's castle and found that all that Blunderbuss had told him was true. He also found the giant's young wife, who quickly got to know and love Tom. Soon the two were married, and they lived for many a long year in the castle by the road.

I Don't Know

Once there was a Duke who lived in Brittany, and he was riding home one day with his manservant when they saw a young child lying asleep and alone by the side of the road. The Duke was curious and sad to see a young boy, about five years old, left by the roadside, so he got down from his horse, went over to the boy, and woke him up.

"Who has left you here, my boy?" asked the Duke.

"I don't know."

"Who are your parents?"

"I don't know."

"Which town do you come form?"

"I don't know."

"What are you called?"

"I don't know."

"Well, no one seems to be taking care of you, so we will take you home and keep you safe." So the Duke took the child home to his castle, and called him N'oun-Doaré, which is the Breton for "I don't know."

N'oun-Doaré grew up in the family of the Duke and proved

to be a healthy, intelligent child. The Duke sent him to school and the lad grew into a handsome young man.

When N'oun-Doaré was eighteen, the Duke brought him back to live at the castle, and, to show N'oun-Doaré how pleased he was with his progress, took him to the local fair to buy him his own sword and his own horse.

First the Duke took N'oun-Doaré to look for a horse. There were many horse-dealers at the fair, but N'oun-Doaré could find no steed that suited him. Then they met a man leading an old mare and N'oun-Doaré shouted, "Yes! That is the horse I want!"

The Duke was surprised. "That old nag?" he said. But the boy insisted.

As the horse's owner was handing over the beast, he spoke quietly to N'oun-Doaré. "You have made a good choice, my boy. Look at these knots in the mare's mane. If you undo one of them, she will fly fifteen hundred leagues through the air."

Then the Duke and N'oun-Doaré went to see the armourer, and looked at many swords. But none was quite right for N'oun-Doaré. Then they came to a junk shop and saw an old, rusty sword. "That is the sword I would like."

"But it's an old, rusty thing," protested the Duke. "You deserve much better than that."

"Please buy it for me in any case, and I will put it to good use."

So they bought the old sword and the lad was pleased. He was even more excited when he looked closely at the weapon and saw that it had a faint inscription, almost covered by the rust. The words "I am invincible" were engraved on the sword.

When they got home, N'oun-Doaré could not wait to try a magical flight with his mare, and before long he was undoing one of the knots in her mane. Off they flew to Paris, where N'oun-Doaré marvelled at the sights of the great city. It chanced that the Duke was also there, for he had been called to attend the king. When he met the boy, they went to the royal palace together. The Duke introduced N'oun-Doaré to the king, and the lad was given a job looking after some of the

royal stables.

One night, N'oun-Doaré was passing a cross roads when he saw something glinting in the moonlight. He found that it was a crown, and that it was adorned with diamonds that shone in the dark. He picked up the crown when a voice said "Be on your guard if you take it." N'oun-Doaré did not know where the voice came from, but it was actually the voice of his old mare. It made N'oun-Doaré pause, but in the end he picked up the crown and took it with him.

He told no one about the crown and kept it secretly in the stables, but two of the other servants noticed it shining through the keyhole and went to tell the king. The king took the crown and called all his wise men about him. But none of them knew where the crown had come from. There was an inscription on the crown, but it was in a strange language and none of the wise men could read it.

Then a small child spoke up, saying that the crown belonged to the Princess of the Golden Fleece. The king turned to N'oun-Doaré: "Bring me the Princess of the Golden Fleece to be my wife, otherwise you will meet your death."

So the lad got on his mare and began his search for the princess, although in truth he had little idea about where to look. As he rode, he came to a beach, and N'oun-Doaré saw a fish stuck on the sand. The creature seemed to be breathing its last. "Put it back in the sea," said the mare, and N'oun-Doaré did so.

"Great thanks to you," said the fish. "You have saved the life of the king of the fish."

A while later they came to a place where a bird was trapped in a snare. "Let the creature go," said the mare, and N'oun-Doaré did so.

"Great thanks to you," said the bird. "You have saved the life of the king of the birds."

Further along on their journey they came to a great castle and nearby a man was chained to a tree. "Set him free," said the mare, and N'oun-Doaré did so.

"Great thanks to you," said the man. "You have saved the life of the Demon King."

"Whose castle is this?" asked N'oun-Doaré.

"It is the castle of the Princess of the Golden Fleece," replied the Demon King. They had reached their goal at last.

They entered the castle and N'oun-Doaré explained why he had come. The princess was unwilling to go at first, but N'oun-Doaré tricked her on to his horse, and away they flew before she could dismount. They quickly arrived back in Paris, where the king wanted to marry without delay.

"Before I marry, I must have my own ring," said the princess.

The king asked N'oun-Doaré to bring him the ring,

and N'oun-Doaré looked about in despair. How would he find it? Then the mare whispered to him, "Ask the king of the birds, who you saved. He will help you."

So they went to the king of the birds and explained that they needed the ring. The king of the birds called all the birds to him. He chose the smallest bird of all, the wren, and told her to bring the ring to the princess. "The wren is the best bird for this task," he explained. "She will be able to fly through the keyhole of the princess's chamber."

Soon the wren returned with the ring, and the king wanted to marry straight away. But the princess had another demand. "I must have my own castle brought to me," she said.

"How shall I ever achieve this?" said N'oun-Doaré in despair.

But the mare whispered to him, "Ask the Demon King, who you saved. He will help you."

So they went to the Demon King, and he called a whole army of demons, and they set to work moving the princess's castle, bit by bit, to Paris, until her wish had come true. The king, of course, wanted to marry straight away, but the princess had a final demand. "I do not have the key to my castle, for it was dropped into the sea when we flew here to Paris on N'oun-Doaré's mare."

N'oun-Doaré saw that this was a task for the king of the fish, who called all his subjects to him. Finally, a fish arrived with

the diamond-studded key in its mouth.

At last, the Princess agreed to marry the king. When the guests arrived they were amazed to see N'oun-Doaré leading his mare into the church. When the king and princess were pronounced man and wife, the mare's skin vanished, and there stood a beautiful young woman. "Please marry me, N'oun-Doaré," she said. "I am the daughter of the king of Tartary."

N'oun-Doaré and the princess set off arm in arm to Tartary. People say they lived happily ever after there, but they were never seen in Brittany again.

The Fenoderee

On the Isle of Man lived a fairy who had been sent out of fairyland because he had had a passion for a mortal girl. The fairy folk found out about his love for the girl when he was absent from one of their gatherings. They found him dancing with his love in the merry Glen of Rushen. When the other fairies heard what he was doing, they cast a spell, forcing him to live for ever on the Isle of Man, and making him ugly and hairy. This is why people called him the Fenoderee, which means "hairy one" in the Manx language.

Although his appearance frightened people when they saw him, the Fenoderee was usually kind to humans, for he never forgot the girl he loved, and wanted to do what he could for her people. Sometimes he even helped people with their work, and used what was left of his fairy magic to carry out tasks which would have been exhausting for the strongest of men.

One thing the Fenoderee liked to do was to help the farmers in their fields. On one occasion he mowed a meadow for a farmer. But instead of being grateful, the farmer complained that the Fenoderee had not cut the grass short enough.

The Fenoderee was still sad at losing his mortal love, and angry that the farmer was so ungrateful, so next year at mowing time, he let the farmer do the job himself.

As the farmer walked along, swishing his scythe from side to side, the Fenoderee crept behind him, cutting up roots, and getting so close to the farmer that the man risked having his feet cut off.

When the farmer told this story, people knew that they should be grateful when the Fenoderee helped them with their work. So the custom arose of leaving the creature little gifts when he had been especially helpful.

On one occasion, a man was building himself a new house of stone. He found the stone he wanted on the cliffs by the beach, and paid some of the men of the parish to help him quarry it. There was one large block of fine marble which he especially wanted, but no matter how hard they tried, the block was too heavy to be moved, even if all the men of the parish tried to shift it.

Next day they were surprised to see that not only had the huge block of marble been carried to the building site, but all the other stone that the builder needed had been moved too.

At first, everyone wondered how the stone could have got there. But then someone said, "It must have been the Fenoderee who was working for us in the night." The builder

saw that this must be true, and thought that he should give the Fenoderee a handsome reward.

So he took some clothes of the right size for the creature, and left them in one of the places where he was sometimes seen. That night, the Fenoderee appeared and found the clothes. Those who watched him were surprised at his sadness as he lifted each item up in turn and said these words:

> Cap for the head, alas, poor head!
>
> Coat for the back, alas, poor back!
>
> Breeches for the breech, alas, poor breech!
>
> If these all be thine, thine cannot be the merry glen of Rushen.

With these words, the Fenoderee walked away, and has never been seen since in that neighbourhood.

A Bride and a Hero

Long ago the Irish believed that there was a faraway land called Tir na n-Og, the Land of Youth. Time went much more slowly there, and people stayed younger much longer. It was the law in Tir na n-Og that every seven years a race was held. All the strongest men of the land took part. The race began in front of the royal palace and finished at the top of a hill two miles away. At the summit of the hill was placed a chair, and the first runner to sit on the chair became king of Tir na n-Og for the next seven years.

There was once a king of Tir na n-Og who was worried that he would lose his kingdom in the next race, so he sent for his chief Druid.

"How long shall I win the race and rule this land before another reaches the chair before me?" he asked the druid.

"Have no fear," replied the druid. "You will rule for ever, unless your own son-in-law wins the race and takes the crown from you."

The king of Tir na n-Og had but one daughter, Niamh, and as yet she was not married. So the king decided that he would

42

keep his kingdom by making his daughter so ugly that no man would marry her. He borrowed his druid's staff, and struck the girl with it, and a pig's head appeared on her shoulders.

When the druid heard what had happened, he was very sorry that he had told the king to beware his son-in-law. He went to Niamh to talk to her.

"Shall I always be like this?" said Niamh to the druid.

"Yes," replied the druid. "You will always look like this unless you go to Ireland and marry one of the sons of Fin."

So Niamh set out for Ireland, hoping to meet one of Fin's sons, and wondering how she could persuade him to marry her. When Niamh had been in Ireland for a while she saw a handsome young man called Oisin, and she was overjoyed when she found out that his father was Fin himself.

It happened one day that Oisin was out hunting, and he and his men hunted further afield, and killed more game than they had ever done before. When Oisin turned to go home, his men were exhausted and hungry, and could carry none of the game home with them, so Oisin was left with his three dogs and a great pile of carcasses.

When the men left Oisin alone, Niamh went up to him and watched him looking at the game. When he saw her approach, the young man said "I shall be sorry to

leave behind some of the meat I have killed today."

"If you tie some of the game in a bundle, I will help you carry it," said Niamh. And off they walked together.

When they had talked for a while, it was clear to Oisin that Niamh was a fine young woman, caring and kind, and it struck the lad that she would probably be attractive too, if she did not have a pig's head on her shoulders. So Oisin asked her about the pig's head, and Niamh explained how she had been told that the only way to get back her own head was to come to Ireland marry one of the sons of Fin.

Oisin smiled. "If that is all it takes for you to get back your

beauty, then you shall not have a pig's head for long," he said.

So it was that Niamh married Oisin, son of Fin. As soon as the ceremony was over, the pig's head vanished, and Niamh's own beautiful face was revealed to her husband. And when he saw Niamh in her new beauty, he loved her deeply.

Soon it was clear that Niamh longed to return to the land of Tir na n-Og, and when she told Oisin of her wish, he was keen to go there with her. He knew that it was the land where people never grow old, and if he went there he would be young for ever. When they arrived at the castle of Niamh's

father, there was great celebration, for everyone had thought that the princess was lost for ever. So for a while the king lived happily with his daughter and son-in-law.

But after a while it was the time for the seven-yearly race to find who should be king. All the likely men in the kingdom, including the king and Oisin, gathered for the race. And before any other competitor was half way up the hill, Oisin was sitting in the seat at the top. No one could deny that it was Oisin's right to be king of Tir na n-Og.

Oisin ruled the Land of Youth for many years, and no one ever argued with his right to be king. He loved his wife dearly, and they were always seen together - in the palace, in the town, or riding their swift grey horse together. Oisin marvelled that he kept his youth, just as did anyone who had been born in Tir na n-Og and lived there all their years. But there was one sadness. Oisin missed his Irish homeland and longed to go back for a visit. He spoke of his wish to Niamh and she turned to him with a warning. "It will be dangerous for you if you return to Ireland," she said. "If you set foot on your native soil, you will lose your youth. You will become a blind old man and you will never come home to me."

Oisin could not believe that this would happen so easily.

"How long do you think you have lived with me in Tir na n–Og?" she asked.

"About three years," replied Oisin.

"But three of our years are like three hundred in Ireland."

Nothing that Niamh could say could change Oisin's mind. He insisted that he wanted to go back. So Niamh decided to help him, in the hope that her husband could hold on to his youth. "Ride to Ireland and do not dismount," she said. "You will only lose your youth if you put your own foot on Irish soil. But if you leave the saddle, the steed will come back to Tir na n-Og and you will be left, old and blind, in Ireland."

With this warning ringing in his ears, Oisin set off for his homeland. The beautiful white horse carried him across both land and sea, and he came at last to Ireland. It was rainy and

windy, but Oisin was happy to be home once more.

Soon he passed a girl and he asked her where he might find the house of Fin and his family. For the land and the buildings seemed changed from when Oisin had last been there. The girl looked at him with a puzzled expression. "I know of no such people," she said. "They do not live around here." And yet Oisin was sure that he was in the right neighbourhood.

He passed other people on his way, and asked each one about Fin and his household of mighty warriors. But no one seemed to know who he was talking about – which was strange, since Fin and his men had been among the most famous in Ireland.

Finally Oisin asked an old man if he knew the whereabouts

of Fin. "I remember my old grandfather talking about Fin and his warriors," said the old man. "They lived in these parts about three hundred years ago."

So Oisin's father and all his family were dead. Oisin could still not believe it. He found the fortress Fin had built, but it was in ruins. He began to believe that what the old man said was true, and that three years in the Land of Youth really were the same as three hundred mortal years.

Oisin decided to seek out the High King of Ireland himself, to tell him of his adventure. As he was riding along the road,

he came across a group of men who were trying to lift a stone. Since he had arrived in Ireland, Fin had noticed that the men seemed weak and feeble compared with those in Tir na n-Og, and these men were no exception. Six of them were tugging away at the stone, but they could not shift it, let alone lift it up into the cart that stood waiting nearby.

Riding up to the men, Oisin called that he would help them. He leaned over to pick up the stone and threw it into the cart, but the effort put Oisin off balance. As he reached out to stop himself falling, one of the stirrups broke and the hero tumbled off his horse and landed on the floor.

As he fell, all the warnings of Niamh ran through his mind. And when he picked himself up from the ground he knew that it was true, he was old, stiff, and blind. He heard Niamh's horse trotting away, and knew that he would never return to the land of Tir na n-Og.

It happened that Saint Patrick lived nearby, and the holy man heard of what had happened. Soon Oisin was brought to Patrick, who gave him a room in his own house, and asked his cook to bring him food every day.

Oisin told Patrick all about his adventures, relating stories about his father Fin and his band of warriors, as well as his adventures in the land of youth, while the holy man listened patiently. Although he was old and blind, Oisin still had a little of his former strength, and sometimes, if Patrick prayed devoutly, Oisin would regain enough energy to help the Saint build his church, and to help rid Patrick of a monster that came to destroy the building before it was finished. But Oisin's strength never lasted long, and soon he would be a weak old man again and it was all he could do to eat the food brought to him by Patrick's cook. And so, old and blind, Oisin lived out the last of his days, with only his memories of Tir na n-Og to console him.

The Lazy Beauty

Once upon a time there was a poor widow who had one daughter. The mother was the most hard-working of women. Her house was neat and clean, and she was especially good at using her spinning wheel to make the finest linen thread.

The daughter was a fine-looking girl, but the laziest creature in the town. She got up late every day, spent hours eating her breakfast, and dawdled around the house doing nothing all day. Whenever she tried to cook, she burned herself, and if she did any other work, she would straight away knock something over or break one of her mother's pots. The girl even drawled her speech, as if it took too much energy to get the words out of her mouth.

One day the widow was giving her daughter a good telling off when she heard the sound of hoof-beats on the road. It was the king's son riding by. When he heard the woman's voice he stopped to talk to her.

"What is the matter? Is your child so bad that you need to scold her so?"

"Oh no, your majesty," replied the old woman, for she saw a

chance to get rid of the girl. "I was telling my daughter that she works much too hard. Do you know, my lord, she can spin three whole pounds of flax in a single day? Then the next day, she will weave it into good linen cloth, and sew it all into shirts the following day!"

The prince reflected when he heard what the woman had to say. "That is amazing," he said. "Surely my mother, herself a great spinner, would be pleased with your daughter. Tell her to put her bonnet on and come with me. We might even make a fine princess of her, if she herself would like that."

The two women were thrown into confusion. Neither of them could have imagined that the old woman's trick would

have worked so well. But quickly enough, the girl had her outdoor clothes on and was lifted up to ride behind the prince. His majesty gave the mother a bulging purse in exchange for her daughter, and off they rode in the direction of the palace.

Now the girl did not know what to do. But it seemed to her that doing little and saying little had served her well to this day, so when she got to the palace she answered briefly and said but few words, in the hope that she would not show herself up as a lazy idiot.

By the evening, she and the prince seemed to be getting on well and the time came for them to show the girl her room. As she opened the door the queen showed her the work she was to do in the morning. "Here are three pounds of good flax. You may begin as soon as you like in the morning, and I shall expect to see them turned into thread by the end of the day."

The poor girl burst into tears as the queen closed the door behind her. She regretted now that she had not listened to everything her mother had told her about spinning, and that she had not taken all the opportunities she had had to learn the craft. She slept little that night with worry and vexation.

When the morning finally came, there was the great wooden spinning wheel waiting for her, and the girl started to spin. But her thread kept breaking, and one moment it was thick, the

next it was thin. She burst into tears as the thread broke again.

At that very moment, a little old woman with big feet appeared in the room. "What is the matter, my fair maiden?" asked the woman.

"I have all this flax to spin, and whatever I do, the thread seems to break," said the girl.

"Ah, if you invite the old woman with the big feet to your wedding with the prince, I will spin your thread for you," the woman offered.

"I will be glad for you to come to the wedding if you will do this work for me," said the girl. "I shall honour you for as long as I live."

"Very well. Stay in your room until evening, and tell the queen that her thread will be ready tomorrow," said the old woman.

And it was all as the old woman had said. The queen came, saw the beautiful thread, and told the girl to rest. "Tomorrow I shall bring you my fine wooden loom, and you can turn all this thread into cloth," she promised.

Of course, this made the girl more frightened than ever, for she was no better a weaver than a spinner. She sat in her room, trembling, waiting for the loom to be brought to her. When the loom was brought, she sat at it and cried once more.

Suddenly, another old woman appeared in the room, a woman with great hips and a small voice, and she asked why the girl was crying.

"I have all this thread to weave, but I cannot work the loom," said the girl.

"Ah, if you invite the old woman with the big hips to your wedding with the prince, I will weave your cloth for you," the woman offered.

"I will be glad for you to come to the wedding if you will do this work for me," said the girl. "I shall honour you for as long as I live."

"Very well. Stay in your room until evening, and tell the queen that her cloth will be ready tomorrow."

Once more, the work was done and the queen was pleased with the cloth. But this time, the girl found herself with the task of sewing the cloth into shirts for the prince. The girl was now in deep despair. She was so close to marrying the prince, but she had no skill whatsoever with the needle. As she sat and cried a third old woman, with a big red nose, appeared in her room. The girl explained her plight.

"Ah, if you invite the old woman with the red nose to your wedding with the prince, I will sew your shirts for you," the woman offered.

"I will be glad for you to come to the wedding if you will do this work for me," said the girl. "I shall honour

57

you for as long as I live."

"Very well. Stay in your room until evening, and tell the queen that the shirts will be ready tomorrow."

So again the work was done, the queen was pleased, and the girl found that preparations for the wedding were being made.

When the wedding came, it was the most lavish feast anyone could remember. The girl's old mother was invited, and the queen kept talking to her about how her daughter would enjoy herself spinning, weaving, and sewing after the honeymoon. Just as she was talking about this, the footman approached the high table and announced another guest. "The princess's aunt, Old Woman Big-foot, has arrived." The girl blushed, but the prince seemed to happy for her to come in. "Tell her that she is welcome, and find a place for her," said the prince.

When someone asked the old woman why her feet were so big, she explained that it was from standing all day working at the spinning wheel.

"Why, my dear," said the prince. "I shall never let you stand all day spinning."

Soon the second old woman arrived at the feast. When she was asked why her hips were so great, she said it came from sitting all day at the loom.

"Why my dear," said the prince. "I shall never let you sit all day weaving."

Finally the third old woman took her place. She explained that her nose had grown big and red from bending down sewing, so that the blood ran always to her nose.

"Why, my dear," said the prince. "I shall never let you sit all day sewing."

So it came about that the lazy beauty never had to spin, or weave, or sew again, and she lived happily in her laziness at the prince's court.

Paddy O'Kelly and the Weasel

There was once a man called Paddy O'Kelly, and he lived in County Galway. Paddy had an old donkey that he wanted to sell, so he got up early one morning and began the journey to market. He hoped one day to be able to buy a horse, though he knew he would not get enough money for the donkey to buy himself a fine steed that day.

Paddy had gone a few miles when it started to rain, so he decided to shelter in a large house. No one seemed to be around, so he went into a room with a fire blazing in the grate. After a while he saw a big weasel come into the room and put something yellow on the grate; then the creature ran away. Soon afterwards, the weasel reappeared, went to the grate, and put down another yellow object. Paddy O'Kelly could see now that these yellow objects were gold coins, and he watched as the weasel came back and forth, every time leaving a guinea on the grate.

When the weasel seemed to stop bringing the coins, Paddy got up, scooped them into his pocket, and went on his way.

But he had not gone far when the weasel ran up to him, screeching and jumping up at him. Paddy tried to beat her off with a stick, but she clung on until some passing men let loose their dog, which chased her away. In the end, she disappeared down a hole in the ground.

Paddy sold his donkey at the market, and used some of the weasel's gold to buy himself a fine horse. He was returning home the way he had come when the weasel popped up out of her hole and attacked the horse. The steed bolted, and ended up nearly drowning in a nearby ditch, until two men passing by helped him pull the beast out. Paddy was exhausted when he got home, so he tethered the horse in the cow shed and went straight to bed.

Next morning, when he went to feed the horse, he saw the weasel running out of the cow shed. The creature had blood on her fur, and Paddy feared the worst. Sure enough, when he got to the shed he found not only his horse, but two cows and two calves dead on the floor.

Paddy called his dog and gave chase, and soon they were catching up the weasel. Suddenly, the creature ran inside a small hovel by the side of the road, closely followed by the dog, which started barking. When Paddy pushed open the door, there was no weasel to be seen, but an old woman sat on a chair in the corner.

"Did you see a weasel coming in, at all?" asked Paddy.

"I did not," said the old woman.

But the dog's instinct was to carry on the hunt, and he leapt at the old woman's throat, making her screech with a noise just like the weasel's cry. Paddy O'Kelly saw that woman and weasel were one and the same.

"Call off your dog and I'll make you rich!" said the woman.

The old woman explained that long ago she had committed a great crime. Her sin would be forgiven if Paddy took twenty pounds to the church to pay for a hundred and sixty masses to be said for her. She told Paddy that if he dug beneath a bush in a nearby field, he would find a pot filled with gold. He could pay for the masses with the money, and use what was left over to buy the big old house where first he saw the weasel.

"Do not be afraid if you see a big black dog coming out of the money pot," she warned. "He is a son of mine and will do you no harm. Soon I will die, and when I die, please do one thing more for me. Light a fire in this hut and burn it and my body together."

Straight away Paddy went to the bush, dug a hole, and found the pot of gold. As he lifted the lid from the pot, a black dog jumped out, and Paddy remembered the old woman's warning.

When he had the money, Paddy replaced his dead cows and horse, and also bought a flock of sheep. He called on the priest to arrange masses to be said for the old woman. And he went to see the man who owned the house where he had first seen the weasel. The owner warned Paddy that the house was haunted, but Paddy insisted on buying it, and stayed in the house all night, until a little man appeared.

The little man, whose name was Donal, made friends with

Paddy. They drank together and Donal played the bagpipes. Donal soon revealed that he was the son of the old woman, and told Paddy that he would be a good friend to him, so long as Paddy told no one else who he was.

Then Donal said, "Tonight I am visiting the Fortress of the Fairies of Connacht. Will you come with me? You shall ride there on a horse provided by me."

Paddy agreed, and at midnight, the two flew through the air on broomsticks that Donal brought with him. When they arrived, the fairy who seemed to be the leader said, "Tonight we are going to visit the high king and queen of the fairies." They seemed eager for Donal and Paddy to go with them, so off they all went.

When they arrived at the hill where the high king and queen of the fairies lived, the hillside opened up for them, and they walked inside. When all the fairies were assembled there, the king explained why they were all gathered together. "Tonight we are to play a great hurling match against the fairies of Munster. The Munster fairy folk always have two mortals to help them, so we would like you to come with us." They set off to the place where they were to play, and the fairies of

Munster were already gathered before them. And so, to the accompaniment of bagpipe music, they began their game.

Paddy saw that the Munster fairies were gaining the upper hand, so he helped the little people of Connacht, turning one of the opponents' human helpers on his back. Once this had happened, the two sides started to fight, and before long the Connacht side were the winners. The disappointed Munster fairies turned themselves into flying beetles and began to eat up all the leaves from the trees and bushes. This went on until the countryside looked quite bare, when thousands of doves flew up and devoured the beetles.

Meanwhile the Connacht fairies returned to their hill, and their chief gave Paddy a purse of gold for his help. Donal took him back home, and he was back in his bed before his wife had noticed that he had gone.

A month went past and Paddy settled down to enjoy his riches, when Donal came to Paddy and told him that his mother was dead. Paddy went to her hut and set fire to it with her body inside, just as she had asked. Once it was burned to the ground, Donal gave Paddy another purse of gold, saying, "This is a purse that will never be empty in your lifetime. I am going away now, but whenever you take money from this purse, remember me and the weasel."

Then Donal was gone, and Paddy and his wife lived long and wealthy, and left much money and a farm to their children. They all did as Donal had asked, and whenever they spent some of his mother's gold, they spared a thought for him and the weasel who had led Paddy to his wealth, when he had gone to sell his old donkey long ago.

The Dream of Owen O'Mulready

Owen O'Mulready was a happy man. He lived with his wife Margaret in a pleasant little house with a large garden. They had enough space to grow all the vegetables they needed, and Owen's master was kind and paid him good wages. Owen had everything he wanted out of his life – except for one thing. Owen had never had a dream. He was fascinated by the tales people told him of their dreams, and he very much wanted to have a dream of his own.

One day, Owen was digging his potatoes when his master came up and started to talk to Owen, as he often did. They began to talk about dreams, and Owen admitted that he had never had a dream, and that he would dearly like to have one.

"I can tell you how to make yourself have a dream," said Owen's master. "Before bedtime tonight, clear the fire from your hearth and make your bed in the fireplace. Sleep there tonight, and surely you will soon have a dream that you will remember for a long while, mark my words."

Owen said he would do this, and when evening came, he

cleared away the fire and made his bed in the hearth, just as his master had told him. When Margaret saw him doing this, she thought her husband had gone mad. But when he explained what his master had said, she let him do what he wanted, for she knew how badly Owen wanted his dream.

So Owen got into his hearth-bed, and soon was asleep. He had not been sleeping for long when there was a loud knock at the door. Owen opened it and a stranger was there. "I have a letter from the master which must be taken to America."

"You've arrived late for such a message," replied Owen. But he accepted the message, put on his boots, and off he went, striding towards the west.

He came to the foot of a mountain, where he met a young lad herding cows. The boy seemed to recognize him, even though Owen had not seen him before. "Where are you going in the middle of the night?" asked the boy.

"I have a letter from my master to take to America. Is this the right way?"

"Yes it is. Keep going westwards. But how will you travel across the water?"

"I will work that out in good time," said Owen. And on he went, until he came to the sea.

Owen found a crane standing on one foot by the shore.

"Good evening, Owen O'Mulready," said the crane, who, like the cow-boy, seemed to know Owen. "What are you doing here?"

Owen explained his business and said that he was puzzled about how to get over the water.

"Sit up on my back, and I will ferry you to the other side," said the crane.

"And what if you get tired before we arrive?" asked Owen.

The crane assured Owen that he would not get tired, and off they went.

They had not flown for long, when the crane started to tire. "Get off my back, Owen, for I begin to tire," said the bird.

"I can't get down now, I'll drown in the water," said Owen.

Owen began to panic, when he saw some men threshing above his head. He shouted to one of the threshers: "Thresher, reach down your flail so that I can hold on to it and give the bird a rest."

The man held down his flail and Owen clung on to it with all his strength. As soon as his weight was off the bird's back, the crane flew off with a mocking cry, leaving Owen hanging in the air.

"Bad luck to you!" Owen shouted at the bird as it vanished into the distance.

Owen's troubles were not over. The thresher began to shout

for his flail. "Let go of my flail, Owen O'Mulready. I cannot get on with my work." Owen protested, saying that he would fall into the sea and drown if he let go, but the man still shouted for his flail, and began to shake the other end, as if trying to make Owen slip off into the water.

Suddenly Owen saw a chance of rescue. A ship had appeared on the horizon, and Owen began to shout and wave with his free hand. Gradually the ship steered towards Owen and still the flail was shaking and Owen thought he might not be able to hang on long enough.

"Are we under you yet?" shouted one of the sailors on board the ship.

"Not quite," replied Owen. The ship came nearer, and the captain began to shout to Owen.

"Throw down one of your boots. If it lands on deck, we shall know we are under you."

Owen kicked one foot, and his boot fell towards the ship. But Owen did not see where it landed.

He was distracted by a terrible scream, and suddenly he heard his wife's voice shouting "Who is killing me? Owen, where can you be?"

"Is that you, Margaret?" asked Owen, not quite sure where he was, or how she had got there.

"Of course it's me," replied Margaret.

Margaret got out of bed and lit the candle. The bed was in a mess and soot was all over the sheets. At first, she could not see her husband, but found him, half-way up the chimney, climbing up and clinging on with his hands. He had on one boot, and Margaret saw that the other had come off and had hit her and woken her.

"So the master was right about your dream," said Margaret, smiling.

"Yes, he was right enough," said Owen.

And Owen O'Mulready never wanted to have another dream again.

The King and the Labourer

A labourer was digging a drain when the king came up to him and began to speak: "Are you busy at your work?"

"I am, your majesty"

"Have you a daughter?"

"I have one daughter and she is twelve years old."

"I shall ask you one question," said the king.

"I am no good at solving questions," said the labourer.

"I shall ask anyway," replied the king. "How long will it take me to travel around the world? Have your answer ready by twelve o'clock tomorrow."

The labourer wracked his brains, but he could think of no way to answer the question. When he got home, his daughter saw that he looked troubled. She asked her father what was the matter, and he told her about the king's question.

"That is not so difficult," she said. "Tell the king that if he sits on the sun or the moon it will take him twenty-four hours."

At twelve o'clock the next day, the king arrived.

"Have you the answer to my question?"

"If you sit on the moon or the sun, your majesty, it will take twenty-four hours."

The king was impressed with the labourer's answer, but sensed that he had not thought it up for himself. The man said that his daughter had told him what to say.

"Here is another question," said the king. "What is the distance between the earth and the sky?"

The labourer could not imagine how anyone could know the answer. So again, he asked his daughter, and she told her father what to do. "Take two pins and wait for the king. When he asks you what you are doing, tell him that you are going to measure the distance from the earth to the sky, but that he must buy you a long enough line, so that you can

make the measurement.

When the king arrived at twelve the next day, the man did as his daughter had suggested.

"That is a good answer," smiled the king. "I do not think that you thought of it by yourself." Again, the man admitted that his daughter had thought of the answer.

"I am impressed with your daughter," said the king. "She must come to my palace to work. If you allow it, I shall be a good friend to you."

So the labourer's daughter went to the royal palace and worked in the kitchens. She worked hard, the king was pleased

with her work, and the girl grew into a tall and beautiful young woman. But because she came from a poor family, the other servants looked down on her and teased her. When the king heard of this, he made her father a knight.

The girl could not believe the king's generosity, but it soon became clear that the king loved the girl and eventually the two were married. Afterwards, the king took his wife to one side and told her that he had something important to say.

"The queen must never speak against the king in any judgement," he warned. "If you do, you must leave the palace."

"It would not be right for me to disagree with you," said the girl. "But if you ever have cause to send me away, please grant me three armfuls of whatever I choose."

"I agree to that," said the king.

And so the king and queen began a happy married life. They soon had a son, which made them even happier, and the labourer still could not believe his luck in being made a knight. One day one of the king's tenants came to the king to complain to him. He had a mare that had foaled, but the foal was always following his neighbour's old white horse, and the man thought that his neighbour was trying to steal the foal. The neighbour, for his part, insisted that the foal was his.

"This is how to solve the question," said the king. "Put the two horses and the foal together near a gap in the wall. Then lead out each horse in turn and see which the foal follows. Whichever horse it follows, her owner shall have the foal."

The king's order was carried out, and the foal followed the old white horse.

When the queen heard what had happened, she went to the wronged owner and told him what to do. "I must not speak against the king's judgement," she said. "But go out and plant some boiled peas near where the king passes. When he asks you if you think they will grow, you can say: 'They're as likely to grow as that old white horse should give birth to a foal.'"

The man did what the queen suggested, and the king saw that he had been wronged. But he also guessed that such a clever ruse had begun with his wife. "Come here, wife," he said. "You are to leave the palace today, for you have given judgement against me."

"It is true that I did so, and I see that I must go," said the queen. "But grant me the three armfuls that I asked for."

The king was angry with her, but there was no going back on his word, so he indicated that she could take what she wanted. His anger turned to astonishment when she picked up both him and his royal throne and carried him outside the door. "That is my first armful," she said. Next, she took the young prince in her arms, carried him outside, and placed him in the king's lap. "That is my second." Finally, she gathered up an armful of all the royal charters and placed them with the prince. "And that is my third. I am happy to leave if these go with me."

The king saw that there was no parting with a woman of such wit. "Oh, dearest of women, stay with me!" he said. They went back into the palace together, and the king ordered that the foal should be returned to its rightful owner.

The Black Lad
MacCrimmon

There was once a young man called the Black Lad MacCrimmon. He was the youngest of three brothers and he was the most down-trodden of the three. His elder brothers were always favoured by their father, and were always given more food, and allowed more enjoyment, than the Black Lad. The Black Lad, on the other hand, was always given the hardest jobs to do when the four were working together.

The father and the elder brothers were all great pipers, and they had a fine set of pipes that they liked to play. The Black Lad would have liked to have played the pipes too, but he was never allowed. Always the brothers took up too much time with their playing to give the young lad a chance.

In those days, people said that the greatest musicians of all were the fairy folk. The Black Lad hoped that one day he would meet one of the little people and they would teach him to master the pipes.

The day came that the lad's father and his two brothers were getting ready to go to the fair. The Black Lad wanted to go too, but they would not take him. So the lad stayed at home, and when they were gone, he decided to take up the chanter from the set of pipes and see if he could play a tune.

After a while of practising, the lad began to pick out a tune on the chanter. He was starting to enjoy himself, and was so absorbed in what he was doing that he did not notice that someone was watching him and listening.

Suddenly a voice spoke in his ear: "You are doing well with your music, lad." It was none other than the Banshee from the castle.

"Which would you prefer," continued the Banshee. "Skill without success or success without skill?"

The lad replied that what he wanted most of all was skill, it did not matter about success. The Banshee smiled, as if she approved of the answer, and pulled a long hair from her head. This she wound around the reed of the chanter. Then she turned to the Black Lad MacCrimmon. "Now put your fingers on the holes of the chanter, and I will place my fingers over yours. I will guide you. When I lift one of my fingers, you lift yours that is beneath it. Think of a tune that you would like to play, and I will help you play. And my skill will rub off on you."

So the lad began to play, guided by the Banshee as she had told him. Soon he was playing with great skill, and he could master any tune that he thought of.

"Indeed you are the King of the Pipers," said the Banshee. "There has been none better before you, and none better shall come after." And with this blessing, the Banshee went on her way back to the castle.

The Black Lad carried on playing when she had left, and he could play all the tunes that he tried. When his father and

brothers returned, they could
hear him playing as they came
along the road, but by the time
they entered the house, the lad
had put away the pipes, and was
acting as if nothing at all had
happened.

None of them mentioned that
they had heard music when they
came in, but the lad's father took
down the pipes, and played as
usual. Then he handed them to
his first son, who played and passed them to the second son.
But instead of putting the pipes away after his second son had
played, old MacCrimmon handed the pipes to his youngest
son. "Now take the pipes, for no longer shall you spend all day
doing the hardest of the work and eating the meanest of the
food."

When the lad played, they heard that he was far better than
any of them. "There is no longer any point in our playing,"
said the father to the two eldest sons. "The lad is truly King of
the Pipers." And the lad's brothers knew that what their father
said was true.

Making a Wife

In the village of New Abbey lived a man called Alexander Harg, and he was newly married. His wife was a fine-looking young woman, and some people thought that if the fairies got hold of her, they would kidnap her, so great was her beauty.

A little while after his marriage, Alexander was out on the shore fishing with his net. Nearby were two old boats, left stranded on the rocks. He did not go too near for he had heard stories of little people being heard around them.

Sure enough, before long, Alexander heard a noise coming from one of the boats as if people were using hammers and chisels in there. Then a ghostly voice spoke up from the other old boat: "What are you doing in there?"

"Making a wife for Alexander Harg," came the reply.

Alexander, astounded and terrified by what he had heard, thought of nothing but running back home to see if his wife was safe. He burst through the door, locked it behind him, and took his young wife in his arms. Then he went round closing all the windows and making sure that no one could get in.

At midnight there came a loud banging at the door. The wife got up to open it. "Do not open the door," whispered Alexander. "There are strange things afoot this night."

So they sat together quietly, and after a while the knocking stopped. But just as they were relaxing again, the animals began to make terrifying blood-curdling noises. The pair of them stayed indoors, and did not open the door until morning.

When they did so, they found a statue, carved in oak, in the shape and likeness of Alexander's wife. The good man made a bonfire and burned the effigy, and hoped never to hear the ghostly voices again.

The Saint and God's Creatures

Long ago, at the time when the first Christians were building their churches in Wales, there lived a young lad called Baglan. He worked for an old holy man, who was struck by the boy's kindness, and his eagerness to serve God.

One day it was cold and the holy man wanted a fire in his room. So he asked Baglan to move some hot coals to make a fire and to his surprise, the boy carried in some red-hot coals in the fabric of his cloak. When the boy had set the coals in the fire, not a bit of his cloak was burned or even singed.

The old holy man knew a miracle when he saw one. "You are meant to do great works for God," said the holy man. "The time is passed when you should stay here serving me." And the old man produced a crook with a shining brass handle and offered it to the lad. "Take this crook, and set off on a journey. The crook will lead your steps to a place where you must build a church. Look out for a tree which bears three different kinds of fruit. Then you will know that you have come to the right spot."

So the young man took the crook and walked southwards a long way. In time Baglan came to a tree. Around the roots of the tree a family of pigs were grubbing for food. In the tree's trunk had nested a colony of bees. And in the branches of the tree was a nest where a pair of crows were feeding their young.

Baglan sensed that this must be the right place. But the tree grew on sloping land, which did not seem good for building. So the young man looked around until he found a nearby area which was flat, and there he began to build his church.

He worked hard on the first day, digging the foundations, and building the first walls, and he slept well after his labours. But in the morning he was dismayed to see that the walls had all fallen down and water was seeping into the foundation

trenches. So the next day, he worked still harder, and raised the walls stronger and higher than before. But when Baglan awoke the next morning, again the walls had been flattened. He tried once more, putting still greater effort into making his building strong. But again the walls were laid low, and Baglan began to despair of ever finishing his church.

Baglan kneeled down to pray, and then he sat down to think. Perhaps he was not building in exactly the right place. So he moved his site nearer the tree, for the holy man had told him to build where he found the tree with three fruits. Straight

away things began to go better. The pigs, rooting with their snouts, helped him dig out the new foundations. The bees gave him honey. Even the crows offered him crusts of bread that they had scavenged. And this time, Baglan's work was lasting.

So he built and built until his walls surrounded the old tree, leaving windows for the pigs and bees, and a hole in the roof for the birds to fly in and out. As a result, his church looked

rather unusual, but he knew that it was right.

The young man kneeled down and prayed to God in thanks. And when he finished his prayer, he saw that all the animals – the pigs, and the bees, and the crows – had also fallen still and silent, as if they too, were thanking God that the work was completed.

After that, Baglan was always kind to the animals, and taught others to show kindness to them also. His crook may have been a holy relic that guided him to the tree, but even it could be used to scratch the back of the great boar.

Jamie Freel

Jamie Freel's mother was a widow, and they had little money to spare. But Jamie was one of the most hard-working lads in his village, and had a strong pair of arms, so they usually had enough to eat. Every Saturday when Jamie came home, he gave his mother all his wages, and thanked her sincerely when she returned half a penny so that he could buy his tobacco.

A short distance from where Jamie and his mother lived was an old ruined castle. The local people said that this was where the little people lived, and Jamie knew that this was true. He himself had seen them, usually at Halloween, when all the windows of the old ruin lit up, and he could hear their music inside the thick stone walls.

The more he listened to the fairy revels, the more fascinated Jamie became. So the next time Halloween came round, he decided to go to the castle, peer through the window, and see what was going on at close quarters.

When the night came, Jamie took up his cap and called to his mother, "I'm just away up to the castle, to see what is going on there tonight."

"Oh Jamie! You don't want to be risking your skin going there," said his mother. "You are all the sons I have got and I don't want to lose you to the little people."

"Have no fear, mother," he called out, making for the castle.

When Jamie looked through one of the castle windows, little people began to notice him, and he was surprised to hear them calling him by name. "Welcome, Jamie Freel, welcome! Come in and join our revels!" they called. And another of their number cried, "We're off to Dublin tonight to steal a young lady. Will you come along with us?"

Jamie liked the sound of this adventure, and was soon flying

through the air at alarming speed with the fairy host. Each town they passed, one of the little people called out its name, and soon the fairy was calling "Dublin!" and they were coming to land in a grand square in the centre of the city. Before long the fairies had kidnapped a young woman and carried her all the way back home.

Now Jamie was a good-natured lad, and the more he thought about this scheme, the more he was anxious for the feelings of the young lady. So when they were near home, he turned to one of the leaders and said, "You have all had a turn at carrying the lady, please let me carry her now." So it was Jamie who was carrying the girl when they arrived home, and he quickly put her down at his mother's door.

When it became clear that Jamie was going to keep the young woman for himself, the fairies grew spiteful. "Is that all the thanks we get for taking you to Dublin?" they screeched. And they tried turning the girl into all sorts of different shapes

– a black dog, a bar of iron, a wool sack – but still Jamie kept hold of her. In the end, when she had regained her own shape, one of the little folk threw something at the girl.

"There's for your treachery," screamed the creature. "Now she will neither speak nor hear." Then the fairy folk flew off to their castle and left Jamie and his mother staring at the poor girl.

At first, Jamie's mother could little think how they would look after a Dublin girl who could neither speak nor hear. But they managed, as they always had done before, and soon the girl herself was helping the widow with the cooking and housework. She even helped outside, feeding the pig and the fowls, while Jamie worked away mending his fishing nets.

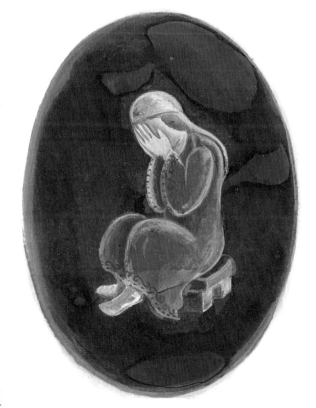

After a year the three had settled down together, although sometimes the girl looked sad and Jamie and his mother guessed that she was thinking of her people and her comfortable home.

When Halloween came again, Jamie decided he would

go and see the fairies once more. His mother tried to stop him, but he was stubborn, and soon he was off across the fields towards the castle.

He crept up to a window and took care not to be seen this time. Soon he heard the fairies talking about what had happened a year before. The fairy who had made the girl deaf and dumb spoke up: "Little does Jamie Freel know that a few drops of this liquid would make her better again."

Now Jamie knew what to do. He burst into the castle and stole the liquid while the little people were still welcoming him. Then he ran home and gave the girl the liquid before anyone could stop him.

The girl was happier now she could talk again, and Jamie and she decided they would go to Dublin to find her parents. After a long and arduous journey they arrived at the girl's family home. But when they knocked at the door, no one recognised her. Her parents insisted that their only daughter had died over a year ago and that they had buried her. Even when she showed them her ring, they would not believe it, accusing her of being someone who had stolen the ring and was pretending to be their daughter.

Jamie and the girl looked at each other. They realised that they would have to tell the people the story of the fairies. It was Jamie who told the story of the flight to Dublin, how the young lady was stolen, and how she had been made deaf and dumb. When he had finished, the old man and woman saw that they had been deceived and that this indeed was their daughter. They showered the girl with kisses – and embraced Jamie, too.

When the time came for Jamie to return home, the girl wanted to go too, for the pair had become inseparable. The girl's parents realised that the two should be married, and sent for Jamie's mother to come to Dublin for the grand ceremony. Afterwards they were all happy, and Jamie felt that all his hard work had been richly rewarded.

The folk tales of the Celtic world capture a world of wistful imagination and earthy humour. Their characters include giants and heroes, noble princesses and honest labourers – and above all, the little people, who promise untold riches, but end up causing mischief wherever they appear.

Celtic Fairy Tales contains a selection of stories from all the Celtic lands – Scotland, Wales, Ireland, Brittany, Cornwall, and the Isle of Man. The tales range from short, amusing anecdotes to lengthier heroic adventures. Enchanting pictures by five of the finest illustrators bring the stories vividly to life. Anyone who loves a good story will love *Celtic Fairy Tales* and return to it again and again.